THE VERY HUNGRY CATERPILLAR

by Eric Carle

Hamish Hamilton. London

Also by Eric Carle

The Bad-Tempered Ladybird
The Mixed-Up Chameleon
The Very Busy Spider
Do You Want To Be My Friend?
1,2,3 To The Zoo
Eric Carle's Fairy Tales and Fables
Brown Bear, Brown Bear, What do You See?
Polar Bear, Polar Bear, What Do You Hear?
Have You Seen My Cat?
The Secret Birthday Message
The Very Quiet Cricket
Draw Me a Star

HAMISH HAMILTON LTD

Published by the Penguin Group
Penguin Books Ltd, 27 Wrights Lane, London W8 5TZ, England
Penguin Books USA Inc., 375 Hudson Street, New York, New York 10014, USA
Penguin Books Australia Ltd, Ringwood, Victoria, Australia
Penguin Books Canada Ltd, 10 Alcorn Avenue, Toronto, Ontario, Canada M4V 3B2
Penguin Books (NZ) Ltd, 182–190 Wairau Road, Auckland 10, New Zealand

Penguin Books Ltd, Registered Offices: Harmondsworth, Middlesex, England

First published in Great Britain
1970 by Hamish Hamilton Ltd

Text and illustrations copyright © 1969 by Eric Carle
20 19

The moral right of the author has been asserted

First published in the United States of America 1969 by The
World Publishing Company, Cleveland and New York

British Library Cataloguing in Publication Data
CIP data for this book is available from the British Library

ISBN 0–241–01798–X

Printed in Singapore

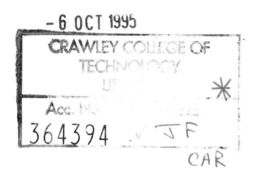

For my sister Christa

Amee

In the light of the moon
a little egg lay on a leaf.

One Sunday morning the warm sun came up and—pop!—out of the egg came a tiny and very hungry caterpillar.

He started to look for some food.

one lollipop, one piece of cherry pie, one sausage, one cupcake, and one slice of watermelon.

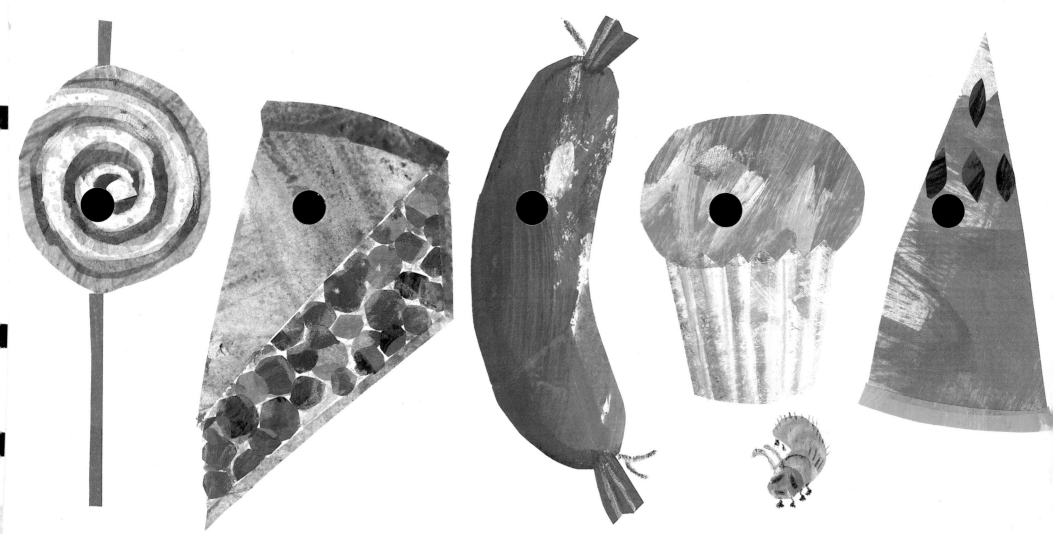

That night he had a stomachache!

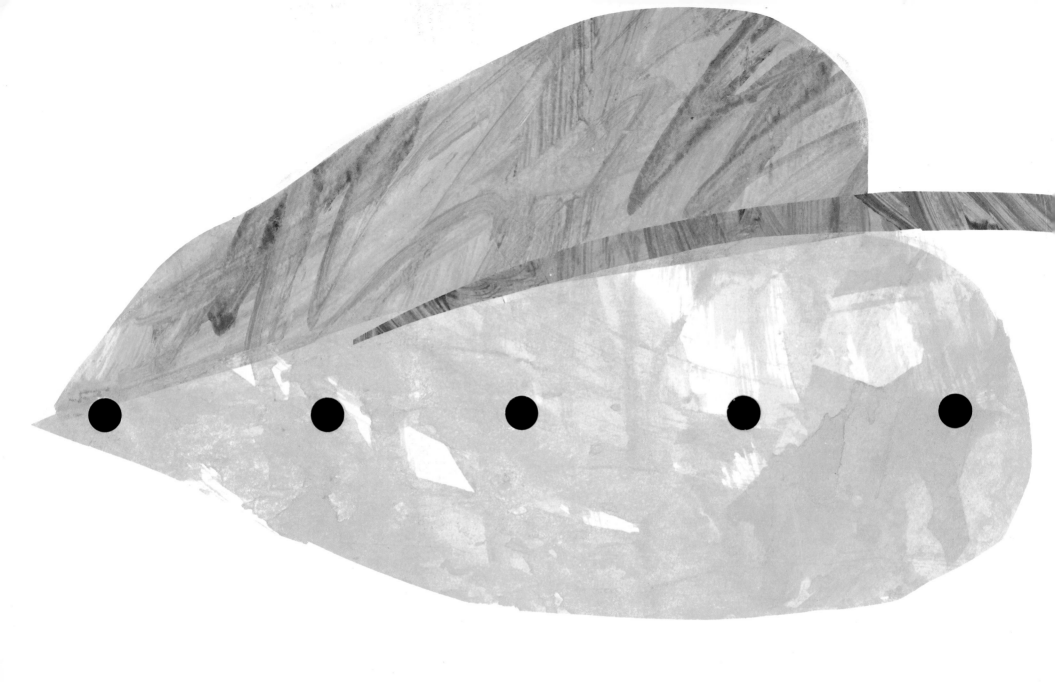

On Friday
he ate through
five oranges,
but he was still
hungry.

On Saturday
he ate through
one piece of
chocolate cake, one ice-cream cone, one pickle, one slice of Swiss cheese, one slice of salami,

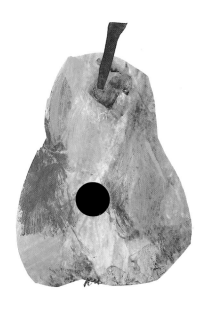

On Tuesday
he ate through
two pears,
but he was
still hungry.

On Wednesday
he ate through
three plums,
but he was still
hungry.

On Thursday
he ate through
four strawberries,
but he was still
hungry.

The next day was Sunday again.
The caterpillar ate through
one nice green leaf,
and after that he felt
much better.

Now he wasn't hungry any more—and he wasn't a little caterpillar any more.
He was a big, fat caterpillar.

He built a small house, called a cocoon, around himself. He stayed inside for
more than two weeks. Then he nibbled a hole in the cocoon, pushed his way out and . . .

he was a beautiful butterfly!